Dear Ichiro

by Jean Davies Okimoto

Illustrated by Doug Keith

KUMAGAI PRESS · SEATTLE

Today everything turned terrible. It happened when my friend Oliver and I were eating Happy Meals and I was showing him my new baseball mitt. Grampa Charlie gave it to me and it has my name, Henry Lockwood, written right in the leather like it was carved in a tree.

"Cool!" Oliver said. "Let me see it!" He tried to grab my mitt but knocked over his grape drink instead, splashing it all over my rabbit, Fang. (I gave Fang a scary name so he would feel brave.) Oliver doesn't know that I still sleep with Fang. He thinks Fang's just some old stuffed animal that lies around like a sock.

"Look what you did!" I yelled.

"Here, I'll wash him off." Oliver yanked Fang away before I could stop him. Then he charged into the bathroom with the grape stuff dripping from Fang's whiskers, covering his face like a big purple bruise.

"Give him to me!" I yelled. Oliver tried to toss him to me but Oliver can't throw, and Fang fell in the toilet.

Oliver laughed his head off at Fang being in the toilet, so I kicked him in the shins. Then he punched me in the nose and we yelled at each other until Mom came and made us both say we were sorry (which I wasn't). Then she fished Fang out of the toilet, sent Oliver home, and gave me a time out. Oliver is the one who should have a time out—for life!

"Use your words, Henry," my mother says when I want to punch someone. Okay, I'll use my words. I AM VERY ANGRY AT OLIVER. He used to be my friend, but now he's my enemy. Here's some more words. Oliver is a snail brain. Oliver is slug slime. Oliver is a bobberty-woop and a blibbity-doop. (Those words are so my mother won't know they're bad words. They're in code.)

While I was having the time out, I made a list of what I would like to do to Oliver.

1. Throw all his baseball cards in the toilet.

2. Put dirt in his chocolate milk.

3. Dump his Happy Meal on his head.

Oliver →

I was so mad I almost forgot Grampa Charlie was coming to take me to the Mariners game. Usually I'd be excited because we both love baseball—which just shows how ruined this day was. Grampa Charlie is my great-grandfather. And he's great all right, and not just because he gives me stuff. (Although I do like the baseball mitt very much. Also the Rollerblades.) Grampa Charlie's my favorite grampa because he listens to me. We also think the same jokes are funny. For example: How is an out-fielder like a frog?

Answer: They both catch flies. Ha!

When Grampa Charlie came to pick me up, I couldn't even think about the Mariners game. All I could think about was how much I hate Oliver. But I hugged Grampa Charlie hard anyway, like I always do.

On the way to the game he told me a new joke. "What did the frog say to the outfielder?" he asked. After I didn't say anything, he told the answer. "Time's sure fun when you're having flies! Ha!"

But I didn't laugh like I always do. I sat like a stone all the way to the game.

When we got to our seats, Grampa Charlie asked me what was wrong. So I told him the whole thing. "I hate Oliver. He's my enemy. I'll hate him forever." Grampa Charlie started to say something, but then "The Star-Spangled Banner" started, so we stood up and sang. He sang really loud, especially the part "the land of the free and the home of the brave!"

Then there was a big cheer as the Mariners took the field, and before you knew it—Bam! Bam! Bam!—the other team was out and we were up at bat.

When our first guy went to the plate everyone chanted his name. "I-CHI-RO! I-CHI-RO!" Ichiro held out the bat like a Samurai sword, then lifted the shoulder of his shirt with his left hand.

"Ichiro's one of the best batters in the game. He's from Japan."

"I know that, Grampa Charlie." Sometimes Grampa Charlie thinks I don't know things.

"A long time ago our countries were enemies," he said, as we watched Ichiro get in position at the plate.

The first pitch was a ball. "I-CHI-RO! I-CHI-RO!" everyone shouted. On the next pitch, Ichiro drilled it into right field and zoomed to first base. He was flying!

Everyone cheered and cheered. Grampa Charlie got
so excited when we jumped up to cheer that he spilled
Coke on his pants, and some got on my shirt.

"Oh shoot!" Grampa Charlie tried to wipe my shirt.
"Sorry about that, Henry."

"Don't worry, Grampa
Charlie. It's just clothes."
(Not like when Oliver
dumped his grape drink
on Fang's head.)

The way both teams kept scoring, I felt like I was on a roller coaster. The whole game was great, and by the ninth inning we were ahead 7 to 6!

There was a huge cheer as the Mariners took the field and our pitcher, Kazuhiro Sasaki, walked up to the mound.

"Watch this guy, Henry. He's from Japan, too."

"I know that, Grampa Charlie."

"He's one of the best closers in the league. That's the pitcher that comes in to end the game."

I sighed. I knew that, too.

Kaz struck out their first three batters—Bam! Bam! Bam! And the game was over! We won!

I was jumping up and down, cheering like crazy with the rest of the crowd, when I noticed that Grampa Charlie had gotten quiet, almost like he was holding his breath. He stared at the Mariners giving each other high fives, especially at Ichiro and at Kaz, whose smile was as bright as sunshine.

"I guess I've come a long way, Henry." Grampa Charlie put his hand on my shoulder. "Sixty years ago when I was in the army, if someone told me there'd come a day when I'd sit in a ballpark cheering for two fellas from Japan on my hometown baseball team, I would have said they were nuts."

"Ichiro and Kaz aren't army guys. They're baseball players."

Grampa Charlie sighed. "I know that, Henry. They weren't even born then, but sixty years ago I thought our countries would be enemies forever, that's all." Then he smiled. "And I never thought I'd see guys from all over the world together on a team like this. It's great!"

Driving home, Grampa Charlie told me his frog joke again. I think he forgot he told it to me before, but this time I laughed as I imagined a frog in a little baseball cap, catching flies. Then I thought about the flies Ichiro caught.

"Grampa Charlie?" I asked, when we stopped at a red light. "You thought you'd be enemies with Japan forever, right?"

"That's right."

"Well, how did things change?"

"I guess it was to the advantage of each country to be friends, to trade with each other and things like that. But also, people wanted to put the past behind them and move ahead. Because basically, Henry," he said, "all people want to live in peace."

When we drove down our street, Oliver was riding his bike in front of his house. He waved at us as we drove by. Grampa Charlie waved back and I sort of wiggled my finger. When we got in my driveway Grampa Charlie opened his door, but I didn't want to go in yet. I looked down the block at Oliver.

"How did that work again? When you quit being enemies?"

"Hearts can heal, Henry."

"How?"

"There needs to be time. Time has to pass."

I looked at my watch. Then I looked down the block at Oliver. "Okay," I said, as I opened my door to hop out.

"Not just time. There has to be goodwill—on both sides. That's the main thing."

"Okay." I jumped out of the car.

"Wait. I'd add something else, too, Henry." Grampa Charlie called after me as he got out of the car.

"Okay." I sighed, waiting for him to catch up to me.

"The hearts have to be in the right position, just like batters have to be in the right position when they get up to bat."

"They do? What position?"

"The hearts have to be open."

When Grampa Charlie left, I hugged him good-bye and thanked him for taking me to the game. Even though the day started terrible, it had turned out good, and before I went to bed that night I decided to write Ichiro a letter.

Dear Ichiro,

I went to the game today and you did great. But that's not why I'm writing you. It's because my Grampa Charlie fougnt against Japan a long time ago and now he's cheering for you. He is so happy you play for our team. And Kaz, too. Since all you guys from different countries can play on a team together, I'm going to try to get along with Oliver so I can play with him. I am going to make up with him just like our countries made up with each other. I might not do it right away though. But probably tomorrow.

Your fan,
Henry Lockwood

P.S. Keep up the good work!

The next day I went over to Oliver's to see if he wanted to play ball. He did, so we went to his back yard. I tried to bat left-handed like Ichiro, and I held the bat out like a Samurai sword and then lifted the shoulder of my shirt with my left hand. But all I did was swing and miss about ten times.

"Maybe if we looked more like Ichiro, it would help." It was muddy from the rain, so I poked my finger in the mud and put a few dots on my face to make a mustache and a little beard.

"That looks good. Put some on me, too," Oliver said.

"Okay." I made a nice beard and mustache for Oliver, and then we tried to hit some more.

We each hit the ball, but mine only went about an inch. Oliver's went two feet and then hit his Mom's flowerpot, so we went to my house and played with my true-to-life dinosaur models.

Before I fell asleep that night, I thought, it's nice to be friends with Oliver again. (I hide Fang under my pillow now.)

And the next time Grampa Charlie takes me to the ballgame, I'm going to ask him if Oliver can come, too.

Baseball: From North America to Japan . . . and Back!

It was practically love at first sight when baseball came to Japan. The game was introduced in the 1870s, during the Meiji Era, when the country was opening up to Western ideas. The Japanese called this new game *yakkyu*, which meant "field ball"—and the more they saw *yakkyu*, the more they loved it. The intensity of the contest between the pitcher and the batter seemed a lot like their martial arts, because it required the athletes to be in top physical condition and have total mental control and split-second timing.

The first professional team in Japan, the Great Tokyo Baseball Club, was formed in 1934, after a team of American stars—including Babe Ruth, Lou Gehrig, and Jimmy Fox—came to Japan to compete with top Japanese college players in a baseball exhibition. In 1936, six other professional teams were formed, and the Japanese Pro-Baseball League was born. The league permitted each team to have four players who were not Japanese, and over the years, more than 500 players have joined Japanese teams from countries such as Korea, Taiwan, China, Brazil, the Dominican Republic, and the United States.

The first Japanese player to come to North America was Masanori Murakami, who pitched for the New York Giants in 1964 and '65. But Murakami was an exception—most players in Japan had a difficult time getting permission to leave their teams until 1995, when pitcher Hideo Nomo was signed by the Los Angeles Dodgers. Nomo became Rookie of the Year and was also named to the 1995 National League All-Star Team. In 2000, Kazuhiro Sasaki signed with the Seattle Mariners and became the American League Rookie of the Year. By 2001, seven Japanese players were pitching for North American major league teams: Sasaki, Nomo, Mac Suzuki, Shigetoshi Hasegawa, Hideki Irabu, Masato Yoshii, and Tomo Okha.

The year 2001 also brought the first Japanese position players to America. Ichiro Suzuki signed with the Mariners and Tsuyoshi Shinjo joined the New York Mets. In Ichiro's first season, he was named to the American League All-Star Team and won the American League's Most Valuable Player, Rookie of the Year, and Golden Glove Awards. Ichiro's 242 hits broke Shoeless Joe Jackson's rookie hit record of 233, which had stood since 1911.

When *yakkyu* was introduced to Japan back in the 1870s, it's a good bet no one would have dreamed that some day Japanese baseball stars would be playing on the major league teams of North America.

Published by Kumagai Press
Printed in Singapore by Star Standard Industries Pte Ltd.
Designed and produced by Sasquatch Books, 615 Second Avenue, Seattle, WA; (206) 467-4300;
www.SasquatchBooks.com; books@SasquatchBooks.com
Design by Karen Schober
Distributed by Publishers Group West
08 07 06 05 04 03 02   6 5 4 3 2 1

Library of Congress Cataloging in Publication Data
Okimoto, Jean Davies.
Dear Ichiro / by Jean Davies Okimoto ; illustrated by Doug Keith.
p. cm.
Summary: After fighting with his best friend and vowing to hate him forever, eight-year-old Henry attends a Seattle Mariners baseball game, where his great-grandfather explains that enemies can sometimes become friends again.
ISBN 1-57061-373-7
[1. Friendship—Fiction. 2. Interpersonal relations—Fiction. 3. Baseball—Fiction. 4. Seattle Mariners (Baseball team)—Fiction.] I. Keith, Doug, ill. II. Title.
PZ7.0415 De 2002
[Fic]—dc21   2002069350

Friends
JE

Friends

jE   Okimoto, Jean Davies
Okimoto   Dear Ichiro

1/2005   ③